OSCAR'S
GREAT
ADVENTURE

Christopher Bailey

ISBN 978-1-64468-288-3 (Paperback)
ISBN 978-1-64468-289-0 (Hardcover)
ISBN 978-1-64468-290-6 (Digital)

Covenant Books, Inc.
11661 Hwy 707
Murrells Inlet, SC 29576
www.covenantbooks.com

Ten percent of net profit from the sale of this book goes to help children in foster care.

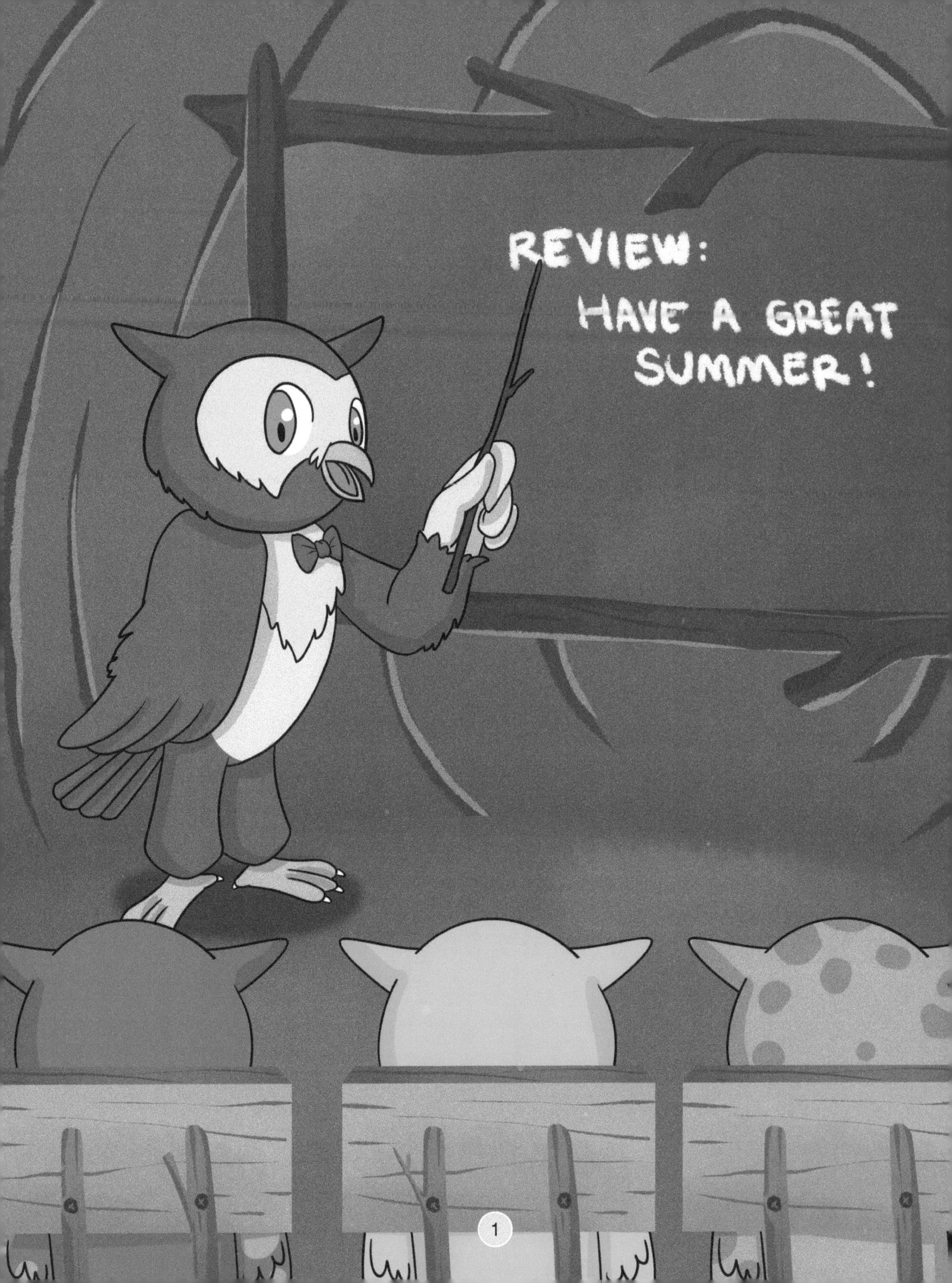
REVIEW:
HAVE A GREAT SUMMER!

Once there lived an owl named Oscar who taught in the forest of Wisenwood. All the creatures of Wisenwood loved to listen to Oscar, for he had much wisdom as an owl should.

On the last day of school, before summer break, a special letter arrived for Oscar.

Dear Brother,
Please come quickly to Woodmont and meet me at my school. We're in great danger from Hector.
Albert

Hector, a mean crow, belonged to an evil hawk named Briar who lived near the swamps. When Briar traveled, Hector became bored and left the swamps to terrorize the creatures of Woodmont.

For two days, Oscar journeyed, but the closer he got to Woodmont, the harder it became to fly. Lightning streaked, the wind roared like a lion, and the trees swayed back and forth.

This isn't good, thought Oscar. *Something's very wrong. It shouldn't be this dark in the middle of the day.*

"Hello! Hello! Hello!"

So Oscar found a safe place to shelter.

Whoosh! A bright light flew around Oscar.

"Oh, my, this lightning is getting worse!" said Oscar. "Wait! This isn't lightning, but what is it?"

"Whooooo are you?" asked Oscar.

"We're fireflies," came a voice floating in front of Oscar's face. "We're here to help you make it through this dark forest."

"I'm most grateful. I can't see as well in the dark as I used to," said Oscar. "What's your name?"

"My name is Blazie. I'm the leader, and everyone follows my light."

Oscar explained his quest.

"We all know about Hector!" winced Blazie. "The forest is so dark, because Hector used a spell from his master's magic book. We'll help you find your way."

With Blazie providing light for their path, Oscar and his new friends arrived at Albert's school.

"Something doesn't seem right," said Oscar. "This looks like a trap."

"Hello, Oscar! We've been waiting for you," came a voice from the shadows.

The room quickly lit up.

"What's the meaning of this? Why is my brother being held captive? What do you want with us?" asked Oscar.

"I want to expand my kingdom," said Hector. "For this, I need your wisdom and knowledge."

"We will not assist you," replied Oscar.

"What do you mean you will not assist? You're the wisest creatures of the forest, aren't you?" asked Hector. "You would be wise to obey!"

"You want wisdom to do bad things, which is not wise at all," said Oscar. "In fact, it's a rather foolish thing. We teach students to do good things."

"Enough!" cried Hector. "I will take your wisdom by use of a spell. When I'm finished, you will both be as brainless as a worm."

Suddenly, Blazie blew out Hector's lamp. The room turned dark. Albert untied the ropes and freed himself.

Albert and Blazie grabbed Oscar and found their way out. Blazie dimmed her light. All the other fireflies turned their lights off. No one could be seen.

When they had reached a safe distance from Hector, they turned their lights back on, one by one.

When Hector lit the lamp again, they were all gone. "Come back, you cowards!" he screamed. "I will teach you a lesson you will never forget!"

Hector began looking for his master's book of spells, but it was nowhere to be found.

"The book! It's gone! I'm powerless without the book of magic! I must find them before they learn my master's secrets!" he screeched.

Hector beat the air with his wings and muttered curses. He flew off to recover the magic book and to destroy Oscar and his friends.

When they came to a nearby river, Oscar dropped the book. It sank to the bottom and the mud quickly covered it.

Suddenly, the skies became clear, and the darkness lifted. All the spells cast by Hector were broken. Not fearing Hector anymore, Oscar and his friends returned to the forest.

"My book! You've destroyed my book!" Hector wept.

"Your terror is over," said Oscar. "Without your evil book of spells, you can no longer scare us creatures of the forest."

Suddenly, Hector's master appeared. All the creatures stepped back and trembled.

"Hector, you played with my magic spells while I was gone, didn't you?" said Briar.

"Please don't be angry with me," pleaded Hector. "I meant no harm. I was only trying to help."

"I'll teach you to mess with my magic book!" cried Briar. "I have one spell remaining, and I'll use it on you!"

With the wave of his wing, Hector lost everything he had learned. He couldn't even remember his name.

"What will I do now?" cried Hector. "I don't even know my way back home, wherever home may be."

"You don't have to go back to the swamps if you don't want to," said Oscar. "I can teach you new things. Sometimes it's good to start over again."

A sad Briar returned to the swamps where he dwelt, powerless.

"Things are looking brighter already!" said Blazie.

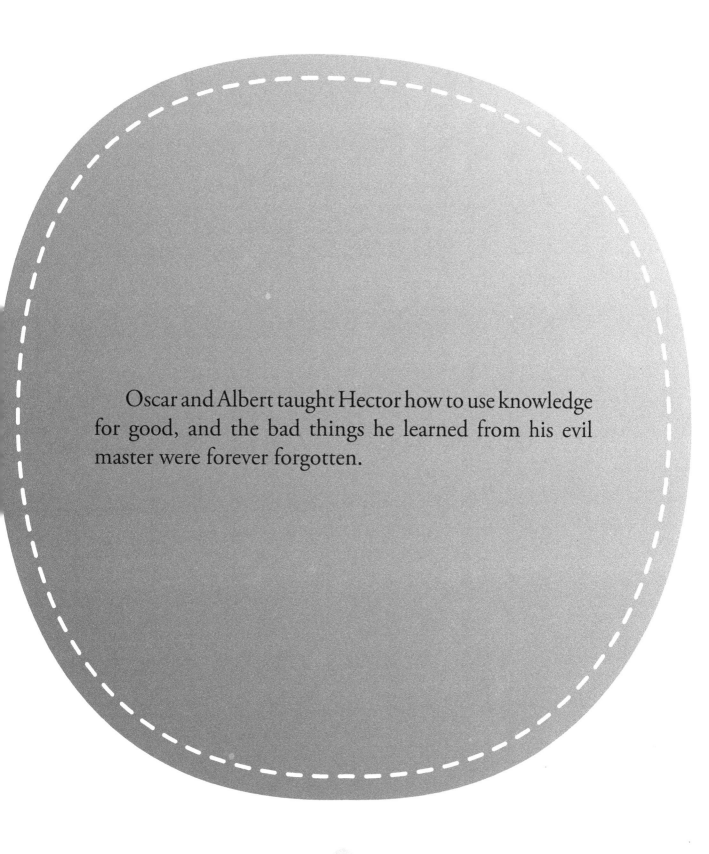

Oscar and Albert taught Hector how to use knowledge for good, and the bad things he learned from his evil master were forever forgotten.

ABOUT THE AUTHOR

Christopher Bailey was born in Monroeville, Alabama. He earned his master of social work (MSW) degree from the University of Alabama where he was also awarded a Master's Scholars Award. He earned his undergraduate degree in journalism from Troy University and is a member of the Society of Children's Book Writers and Illustrators.

An adoptive parent, he is a licensed social worker and has worked with children in foster care for more than a decade. *Oscar's Great Adventure* is his debut picture book.